WOLF DESIRES FIRST BITE

PARANORMAL EROTICA

CANDRA AUBREY

plicit Press
Erotica Fiction

CHAPTER 1

I ALWAYS GOT what I wanted. It was like a natural thing for me to do so. After all, as the daughter of one of the wealthiest people in town I knew that regardless of who it was I was dealing with, I would always get the upper hand and I would definitely get the best thing that I could get out of any deal. Whether it be clothes, shoes, boys, or even the schools that I went to, I knew that regardless of what happened, I would be able to really get what I wanted and nobody could stop me.

That was the thing. I was so popular that the idea of even stopping was something out of the question. Nobody tried to walk into my territory. As one of the most popular kids in school and as one of the prettiest ones, I know for sure that I certainly got the best results and the best things that I could. Nobody defied me. Instead, they all worshipped me like I was the leader that they wanted. And dammit I would certainly give them that satisfaction.

It felt so good to lead. I was never a follower. Even in grade school, I never did that thing called "following orders". I was always a troublemaker, and that trait continued on for a long time. Even in high school, I never gave a damn about what others thought. It was only when the threat of being cut off happened that I started to shape up and soon my grades went from Ds to As all around. Of course, I did use my sex appeal to help get my grades up. Teachers could never say no to a hot chick like me who was willing to do anything for a little bit of fun. And I know that they liked my body, for they would drool over it day in and day out.

I worried occasionally. Sometimes a couple of girls would come by and they would try to challenge me. It was quite cute actually, but they never seemed to beat me. It was then when they would realize just who I was and then shut up, for they all knew that I was the one in charge here and not them. It only took a couple of tries to get the point across with most of them, which was always a good thing and one of the reasons why I was able to do whatever I want and get whatever I want.

"Man it's good to be me," I said aloud as I entered the party. When I got in there dozens of people knew who I was. After all, how could they not? I was gorgeous, and they immediately put two and two together once they saw me. It was cute actually, for they knew that I was the type of girl who was going to give them a great time.

The party was pretty lame, but I was going through drink after drink. It was like the men begged to pour me them, and soon I was at five shots and three martinis. I could feel my body start to get a little bit woozy just thinking about everything, and after a while, I knew that it was time to get home. Maybe I was becoming a lightweight in my time at this school due to my desire to study and work hard in order to get what I really wanted. If that was the case, then I would hate to see just how much of a party pooper I was going to become eventually. I hated to think about it, but I know that someday I was going to have to stop. But until then I was going to continue my pathway and have fun.

As I was about to walk out one of the guys came by. Even though I was a bit hazy, I knew automatically that it was Doug, one of the creepiest guys in school. He was this chem nerd who wanted nothing more than to get in my pants. And I know that he did, I read his journal once as part of a peer session for class once and I left more disgusted than I had ever felt before. He really wanted me, and I know that In my drunken stupor he would try something.

"Hey Farah, want to—"

"Piss off Doug. I don't want you!" I cried out to him. It was a lot louder than I expected it to be. I was probably too drunk to realize that the sound of my voice reverberated through the room. He immediately backed off after I punched him in the balls, and he doubled over in pain. Instead of people coming to his aid though, they laughed at him. I laughed too. It was funny to watch.

I walked out and started to fumble with my phone, and then after a while, I dropped it somewhere. I started to walk down the street. Even though daddy hated it when I didn't take the limo home, I didn't need that fucking thing tonight. I would be fine on my own. Or at least I thought.

I started to walk down the way and then I saw a guy in a hoodie sitting on a bench. He looked like he was waiting for something, and I wanted to know what it was. After all, he did look pretty damn cute. After a second or two though, he got up, and then he started to walk toward me. This was getting really fucking weird.

"Umm hi?" I asked aloud. I didn't know what else to say besides that.

"Hello there. Are you Farah?"

"Y-yeah. But why do you want to know?" I replied. I started to act all tough, even though I barely knew where the hell I was. I hated being so drunk, but I know that I did that to myself. That's the punishment that I get for getting wasted at some shitty party. However, I still had a bit of a hold on reality, even though I felt like I was walking and talking through a haze the entire time. I couldn't shake off the feeling, and after a minute or two, he responded.

"Come with me. I need to show you something. It's very important. Your father wanted me to give you this," he said.

I wondered what the hell he was getting at, but if my dad ordered it, then it can't be all that bad right? I didn't see why not. I started to follow him into the forest nearby, trying to shake the feeling of nervousness that this man seemed to continue to give me. He didn't feel safe, and as I walked with him I started to feel even more ill at ease than I had ever felt before.

I wanted to know where we were going, but I didn't want to piss him off. I guess the best way to find out was to just walk, and that's what I did. I continued to trudge through the forest, the alcohol still in my system, but starting to get weaker as I walked. Maybe I was metabolizing it or something. I didn't really fucking know at this point.

When we got to the middle of the forest, I looked around. It was completely dark and a part of me felt like this wasn't the place I was supposed to be in. That my dad really didn't want me here, and that this was all just a lie. I wanted to tell him that, but before I could he smiled at me and started to say a few words.

"Oh gods that are among us, I have brought the sacrifice

to you. I knew that this is more than you expected," he said in a low voice.

"Sacrifice?" I asked aloud as if this was something that I had never heard before. Which it wasn't, except in the area of movies and video games that I would play with my boy toys. But this was different, this man didn't look like he was playing a game. However, before I could ask any more about it and try to figure out what to say, there was a low growl.

"What the hell was that?" I asked aloud. The man simply smiled, and soon he started to walk away, fading into the shadows.

Soon the creature got closer, and I could hear his footsteps in the darkness. It sounded like a wolf, but I didn't know. I was still too inebriated to really function at this point. But before I could ask, the creature jumped out and pinned me down, leaving me there to struggle. I tried to move, but it was no use. This creature was taking me down with him, and I was going to get pinned to the ground and be at his mercy.

He started to swipe at me, tearing off my dress and undergarments. I was soon naked, but I didn't give a shit. If this was someone's idea of a sick fucking joke this needed to stop because there was no way I could allow this to happen to me or to anyone else. I had to get the fuck out of there, and soon I started to run. Where I was going, I didn't really care. I had to run.

I started to go through the maze of trees. I didn't even know where I came from anymore. The trees were so similar that it was like I was getting lost in a giant maze that I couldn't get out of. I could hear the footsteps following me, and soon I started to run faster. The creature picked up the pace and I could hear it after me. However, after about another five minutes or so, I stopped, trying to catch my breath. There was no sound around me, and I definitely didn't like the feel of that. He could be anywhere, but after another minute or so of not hearing him, I decided to think that he was gone for good.

"Thank God that's over," I said aloud. This was getting way too damn weird for me, and I needed to get the hell out of here as fast as I possibly could.

I started to walk a little bit when I suddenly heard the howl once again. This time it was right in front of my face, and I turned. I could see the wolf in the haze of the outline, and I know that he was definitely hungry for something. I could almost see the visual of the creature licking his lips when he saw me, and that sent terror shooting through my body.

"Fuck," I said aloud. I didn't want to be another person's snack, but what else could I do? I was trapped, and this wolf creature was definitely not going to let me get away. I was stuck here, and I know that it definitely was not going to be easy to get out of.

He lunged at me, pinning me to the ground instantly. I didn't know what to do at this point, so all I could do was scream. I don't get why I screamed, but I just did, but the screams started to get weaker and weaker as the creature pinned me down. I could feel it puncture one of my lungs, and a part of me wondered if that was how I was going to die, by being choked to death and by a punctured lung.

However, after a moment or so the creature came close to my shoulder and bit it hard, eliciting another painful scream from my lungs. It was the only one I could muster, and the wolf seemed to like it. He continued to bite down harder and harder, and I continued to scream until I didn't have any air left in my body. That was a scary thought, but I didn't know what to do about it. I was trapped, and this wolf loved the way that I looked. He seemed to get off on the feeling of pain, almost like a sadistic human when they see someone in pain and whom they want to torture.

After another minute or so the wolf finally got off of me, but it was too late. I could feel the blood oozing out of my skin, and I could feel it trailing around my brown hair. This wasn't how it was supposed to end, was it? To be killed by some motherfucking animal who didn't know his ass from his head? That wasn't the way I was supposed to go. I was the daughter of a fucking billionaire for Pete's sake! Yet, as I sat there I knew that it was the end. There was no way out, and there was no way to get out. I was trapped, like an animal in a cage that wasn't able to get free from it and go back to its master. I hated it, but that was the way shit went down in my life I guess.

"I guess... this is how it ends," I said aloud. The wolf waited until I was dead before walking away, and as I closed my eyes, I saw it walk, and for a moment I could've sworn that it did something I thought that It would never do in a million fucking years. No way, no how.

It turned into a human.

CHAPTER 2

I WAS SUPPOSED to be dead.

At least that's what I thought. I seriously thought that I was a goner. I mean shit, how could I survive a punctured lung and a deep bite in the shoulder? I know that I died of blood loss, but as I started to rouse a little bit I started to realize something. This wasn't heaven, nor was it hell. I don't think it was purgatory, because I don't think in purgatory they chain you up and they leave you there. No, this was something else. I was pretty sure I knew what it was, and that's what scared me even more than anything else in the room.

I was alive, and this was earth. I was still here, and I wasn't in some afterlife that other people claimed there was just to make a quick buck.

I never thought that there was from the start, but thinking about the afterlife did make me wonder a few things. I always did wonder where I was going to go when I died, but I didn't know for sure. However, as I sat there I realized that I was still myself. I wasn't some sort of fucking angel or anything. I was a real human, and I wasn't dying or dead.

What weirded me out even more so, however, was the fact that my injuries were gone. I could breathe normally, and my heart rate seemed about as normal as it could be. I was very hot though, so a part of me was worried that I might be in shock or something. But after a bit, I seemed to calm down as I stood there.

I was chained to the wall, and instead of being fully dressed or even naked, I was just in a simple bandeau top that clasped at the back like a bra and a small piece of underwear. Hell, I don't even know if this shit would count as underwear at this point because of how small it was, but frankly, I didn't give a shit. At least I wasn't naked.

I stood there with the chains on and wondered just what the hell was going on. Why in the world was I being taken like this, and why was I being tortured like this. I didn't know why, but damn, I was getting tired of just laying here.

As if my prayers to finally get answers came true, the door started to open just a little bit. It started to inch a bit more until two men came in. They both had smiles on their faces as they walked toward me.

"Look at what the alpha got. Nice job," one of them said.

"Thank you. But she's both of ours. We will both take her at the right time. I think we should wait until the ceremony," he replied. The other man had a very low one, but the guy who just spoke was even lower than that one. It sounded like two black men, but they were both white, which was a bit shocking. Those men would do great as soul singers.

They started to move closer and I grimaced at them. I

saw the look on their faces, and that was lust. It was definitely that feeling, and I automatically froze. There was no
way these fuckers were going to touch me, not if they were
the last two men on earth.

After the second one of them came over to me and
started to breathe into the shell of my ear, sending shivers
down my body. I really didn't want it to, but I couldn't help
it. In a very weird and fucked up way, I was turned on just
by hearing it. I wanted them, and I could tell that they
wanted me just as badly. I immediately went from hating
them to loving them as they started to lick the shell of my
ear, sending jitters through my body. They started to move
their hands toward my mouth and start to trace circles
around the edge of it. I didn't know what the hell was going
on, so I sat there frozen and wondering what to do.

"God, I can't hold back. I want her so fucking badly,"
one of the men said. It was the one that said something
about the alpha thing before. Which made me wonder what
he was saying as well. Alpha stuff sounded like a sorority
thing or a frat thing. Yet these boys didn't look like any
brothers that I know of. Were they from a rival school and
doing this to weird out mine? It wouldn't be the first time
I've heard some people go to really fucking desperate
lengths just to get a rise out of our team. And most of the
time it did. That had to be the case because they know that
they decided to kidnap the most popular girl in school, and I
know that they're just doing it as a scare tactic at this point.

"What are you doing? You know that you can't hurt
me," I said aloud.

Instead of an answer, I get a slap across the face. It
stung, but at the same time, it felt good. I don't even know
why it did, but I liked it a whole lot. I wanted them to slap
me again for some reason.

As if reading my mind, the other man slapped me a bit softer this time. However, it still stung and made me moan like crazy as he did it. It was really hot, and I felt really excited just at the idea of him doing that. I wanted more, and judging by the look on their faces, they knew that I wanted them to do it again.

"Look at the little slut. She likes it so much that she wants us to do it again."

"I think we should," one of them replied.

I looked at them and gulped. They started to move closer to me with their mouths, each of them inching over to my body and making me gasp a little bit. I hadn't been this close to a guy in a while that I thought was kind of sexy. These guys were built like Adonis, and I definitely liked that. They weren't like the jock fags that I saw all the time in class or at parties. These were real men, not boys,

They started to get closer until they were each right by the corner of my mouth. Instead of kissing me one at a time, though, like I expected them to, they then started to kiss me with their tongues at the same time, pushing my mouth open and forcing their tongues into my mouth and mingling with mine. It was really sexy, and I couldn't help but moan a little bit as I felt them against me. It really did feel good, and already I could feel the wetness pouring into me. Even though I didn't like the fact that random guys were touching me, it didn't bother me because they were hot. I was still a bit scared though, but it was almost like they took the fear away a little bit and replaced it with wanton pleasure.

They started to kiss me harder and harder, each of them snaking their hands up my sides to one of my breasts, touching it softly. I moaned, my body loving the way it felt. It was a very muffled moan due to the two tongues in there.

After a bit though they pulled away and smiled, both of them excited for what was to come next.

"Do you think we should use our hands or our tongues?" one of them asked. I didn't know if they were talking to me or the other guy, but I definitely wanted them to touch me more with their tongues. It felt like two snakes slithering across my skin, and in a very odd way, it really did turn me on a whole lot and got me excited as well.

"I think we should use our tongues. I would love to taste her down there," the other replied.

I gasped as they started to move the muscle down my neck and to where my breasts were. They quickly did away with the bandeau, throwing it on the ground and leaving me topless. They quickly move their tongues over each of the nipples, caressing them with it. I moaned at the feeling, my hips lightly bucking. I wanted to move more, but the chains restricted me as they continued to kiss and lick all over the two sensitive buds and causing them to harden even more than they were before. It felt so good, and already I know that despite my desire to not go so far, they would send me over the edge.

They made their way down, but instead of both of them going for my pussy, I was in for a very interesting moment. They started to pull down my panties slowly but surely. It was almost painful for them to do this, for I could already feel the pleasure starting to course through my body as they did this, and while they continued to do that I wanted them to touch me even more. They finally made it to each of the sides with their tongues, but one of them took the front while the other took the back. It was definitely different, and at first, I flinched when the one man was right by my back hole. I had never done anal before, and I was scared to do it, but soon he started to flick his tongue over my entrance and I moaned in pleasure. The other man made his way down to my pussy and started to lick on my clit, making the rimming behind me even more pleasurable. I was moaning even louder than before, and the guys certainly got a satisfaction out of it. It was like they wanted to see me like this and the fact that I was going this nuts already told them that tonight was going to be a whole lot more fun than they ever expected it to be before.

They continued to lick at me, while the one guy also started to finger my ass while the other man started to finger my pussy while playing with my clit. I was already breathing heavily, and the string of moans that came out sounded like music to their ears. They loved seeing this side of me, but I know that they wanted more. It might have been fun teasing me with oral, but I could tell that they were ready for something else.

However, the one behind me wanted to prepare me more. He started to slip a second finger into me, replacing his lips with the finger and stretching me out. I moaned in pleasure as I felt this, my body going crazy with lust and desire. I didn't know how nice it felt, and the man behind me didn't realize it either until just now.

"Wow, you really love your little asshole getting played with don't you? You're the perfect little slut for the alpha then. I'm glad they found you in the forest," he said. I wanted to find out about the forest, but I didn't know if this was a bad idea or not. They started to pull away, and I heard the sound of them unzipping. After a moment, I saw their cock, and boy was I surprised.

They were big, and that was saying something. I always had a personal love for the bigger ones, but these were massive. I never thought I would see such big cocks in my life, but they were there and throbbing. They both had to be about ten inches, and I know that this was going straight into me.

They pulled up my legs and I held suspended in the air. It was a bit scary, but I didn't know what to do about it. However, after a second, they started to push into me, and already I could feel my body start to tense up and go mad with pleasure.

They started to push deeper and deeper into me, filling me up with their giant cocks that made me feel amazing. They started to move in and out of me slowly at first, but then faster and faster, causing me to moan in pleasure at these feelings. It was amazing, and I definitely could feel the passion start to get even stronger with each thrust.

They started to move at different times, and I know that I was at my limit. I was on the edge, and they both knew this. However, they wanted to see how far I could go. They started to move at fast speeds, and I definitely could feel my body going crazy with passion. After a few more thrusts, I knew I couldn't take it anymore, and they were definitely going to come with me as well.

I felt the man in the back come first, filling up my butt with his seed. The guy right after me moaned as well, and I could feel his cock twitch inside of me as he came. It felt good, surprisingly, and I know that I was definitely going to come right after. I felt the muscles in my body tighten up as I gasped in pleasure, trying to catch my breath and get air as I rode out my orgasm. It felt amazing, and they were definitely happy as well.

After they finished up, and after that they pulled out of me. I had a very tired look on my face, and they smiled at me with a look of pleasure.

"Looks like the new mistress loved it. Let's just leave her

alone so that she can get ready for what's about to come next," the man said.

The other chuckled and walked away, leaving me all alone. I can't believe what just happened. These men took me, and even though I didn't like it at first, I did enjoy it at the end. However, I did feel battered and tired and didn't know what to do with myself. I fell asleep as best as I could against the wall, wondering what was to happen next.

As I lay there, I heard the door open once again and another man came in. This guy was different from the others, but I could tell that he had the same wanting look on his face. It was a bit creepy to think about, but I wasn't going to get into that right now. He came over and walked up to me, and after a second, he sniffed me.

I looked at him with the biggest "what the fuck" face ever. Why the hell was this guy sniffing me? And why did he look at me with a look of sheer pleasure on his face after that? Something was up, and I didn't know what to do about it. After a moment or two, he spoke once again.

"My you're nice. I bet they had a lot of fun with you," he said.

I steeled myself for what he was about to do next. I don't think I could handle another fucking right now. However, he just lightly touched my hair and looked at me with a smile. This guy was different, but I didn't know if I could trust him or not.

"What? You're going to fuck me too?" I asked aggressively. That would get the point across if he planned to do any such thing.

"Not at all. I just came to check up on you. I know that you recently turned so I didn't know how you were handling everything," he said very calmly.

I wanted to ask him more things, but there was one

thing that got my attention that definitely made me worried. The idea of him seeing me turn... what did that all mean and why was he saying such a thing.

"What are you talking about? Turning? What am I fucking doll or something?" I asked.

He looked at me with wide eyes, a shocked expression plastered on his face. Well, I guess that makes two of us.

"You don't know?"

I looked at him with a worried glance. Of course, I didn't know, I don't know why I was being tormented like this either.

"No. What's going on?"

He sighed and looked at me, and I could tell that something was amiss. He definitely looked worried, and I know that I had to ask him. Even though I didn't trust him, he seemed friendlier than the two horny boys from before.

"Well, you did die, but now you're alive again. You're a half-wolf, half-human. And you're part of a prophecy that's going to come true very soon."

CHAPTER 3

I THOUGHT HE WAS JOKING. There was no way this was true. I can't believe it, and when I heard this, I immediately grew nervous and started to shake my head.

"You have got to be shitting me."

"I'm not. I mean it. You were a human, but you're now a human and a wolf. Do you remember when you died?"

I thought about it. I did die, but I don't remember anything about any wolf bullshit. This guy had to be fucking high.

"Just me dying. I don't remember any of this wolf shit."

"That's because you were drugged after. You have turned, and we had to watch the turning to make sure that you're okay. However, since you are, you're now free to go. But you should watch out. You're in great danger Farah, and I think you should keep one eye open and look behind you when you're alone," he admonished.

This guy had to be joking. Why should I worry so much? I don't get what he's getting at, but I'm not going to try to understand him.

"Thanks, but no thanks. I just want to leave."

The man nodded, and in a weird way, he seemed to understand the pain that I was going through and my inability to understand or believe anyone's bullshit right now.

"I understand. Just know that I'm not lying to you."

I nodded and just tried to get this all out of my head. He handed me a black dress, and it looked more like a robe when I put it on. I gathered the underwear from before and put it on with the dress and walked out. Maybe now I could leave this nightmare for the real world and get back to my normal life. That's all I wanted anyway.

The next couple of weeks were normal. I was a college kid, my parents worried about me, and I definitely had my own share of fun. I went to one of those parties the track kids throw each year about three weeks later, but it was boring as shit. I didn't want to get wasted because after what happened the last time I did want to have my wits around me. However, I was still a bit buzzed and that helped calm me down.

I was about to leave when I saw the one person that I thought I would never see. It was him, the captor that I fucked. That was the one who fucked me in the ass, and when he saw me, he immediately smiled. This was different from last time, but he definitely did like the way that I looked. I tried to run away, but going through a throng of people was hard. Soon he caught up to me, and just as I was about to run out the back door, a hand caressed my shoulder. I turned around, and it was him. Instead of his expression from earlier, he had an apologetic face.

"Hello there. We need to talk."

CHAPTER 4

WHY THE HELL would I want to talk to him? I mean fuck, he bound me and then fucked me in the ass. Why the hell would I want to talk to the scumbag who took my anal virginity? That was disgusting.

"Why should I talk to you?" I asked in a very rude manner. It was probably a bit harsh, but this whole thing was so messed up that I needed some space and a chance to think about things. It was still hard even mentioning it to myself, let alone thinking about it for a very long period.

"I have to tell you a few things. It's about what Quinn said to you earlier," he said.

I wondered who Quinn was but then I put it together. He was the nice one, the one who didn't fuck me.

"What? You want to say how sorry you are for fucking me in the ass?" I retorted.

"Well, that, but there are other things as well," he replied.

I huffed, but then walked with him over to where the private area was. He stopped and then pushed me up the stairs to one of the bedrooms. We avoided the one with the

string of moans coming out of it, but then we took the unoc-
cupied one. I wasn't trying to push anything on him, but I
know that I definitely liked him despite what he did. In
addition, I wanted to get the answers that I wanted to know
and I wanted to figure all this shit out for myself before it
was too late.

He sat down and sighed, and I looked at him with a very
anticipatory glance. He looked at me for a second before
talking to me.

"Sorry about what I did. I was forced to. I mean, don't
get me wrong, you're sexy, but you definitely looked scared.
I didn't want to fuck you in the pussy that time, so that's
why I took the backside. Plus, I'm not an alpha yet, so I do
want to make sure that I don't hurt you before that," he said.

"What do you mean about the whole alpha thing? I
mean I heard that a lot, and not just from you. The other
guy said it too."

"That means the alpha wolf, the leader of the pack.
There is a fight going on and I'm supposed to be the leader.
But there is a lot of drama. I don't want to get you involved
though," he replied.

I got a bit annoyed by that. I mean wasn't I already
involved by just being here and listening to this bullshit.

"Well, it's already too late for that. I'm in too deep, and I
know that regardless of what you say I'm going to have to
get involved in some fashion or another," I replied.

"Well, I do like the fact that you care. Still, I'm a bit
scared about it. I mean I've never gotten someone involved
in my life before. But I know that you do care because if you
didn't, you wouldn't be here listening to me talk about all of
this," he replied.

As much as I didn't want to say it, that was the truth.
Even though I hate what he did, I know that he was a good

man. Besides, he did have the decency to apologize, and that was better than the dipshit exes that I had to deal with in the past. This guy was all right, and I definitely wanted to find out more about this.

"It's okay. I know you had to do what you had to do. Now, what do you mean about the whole mistress thing? I mean, I don't think my dad would be too happy with me running off with some wolf guy or something," I said.

"Well, that's the way life is. The problem is, they've already chosen a mistress for me, so I have to go along with the choice despite my desire not to. It's not that I want to, but it's more that I have to. I'm forced to live this life, and this was the life I've chosen. As much as I want to give you a chance, I don't know if I can," he replied.

I didn't like the sound of that. First of all, my dad was going to piss himself along with probably kill every male in a five-foot radius if he found out I was going off and fraternizing with guys who didn't have any prestige or privilege. Plus, I know that he wants me to continue in school. There was no way that I could if I was a mistress! That would make it completely impossible.

"Why do I have to do this? I mean, I know that I don't want to upset people, but I definitely don't like the sound of this," I asked.

"It's because you were chosen. But I'm not going to force you. You can come whenever you want to. Despite the fact that they might get annoyed, I don't see the point in forcing you. Besides, you are a free woman so you can decide whatever you want."

"True," I replied. I did have my own choice, and I didn't know for sure what to do yet. But I definitely wanted to find out more about it. It didn't seem like such a bad offer anyways.

"I mean, I'm willing to see what it's like and stuff," I said.

"Well, I'm not going to force you. However, I do want to give you something that I feel like I should've given you the first time properly, but I got pushed out of the way before I could do such a thing," he said.

I wondered what it was but before I could ask, his lips were on mine. This time it wasn't some sickening and passionate kiss, but it was a friendly one made of love and happiness. It was nice to feel, and I lightly moaned in pleasure as he kissed me softly. It felt good, and as I moaned, he started to lightly capture my mouth with an even deeper kiss than before, causing me to lightly gasp in the pleasure that I felt as I did this.

We continued to kiss each other hard for a little bit, both of us moaning in pleasure at the feeling. His thing pushed his tongue in, causing me to moan at the way he mingled it with my own. This felt different from last time, for this time it actually felt good when he did this. We continued to mingle our tongues together, both of us moaning in pleasure at the feeling that we got. He then pushed me down on the bed and hovered over my body, smiling at me.

"Let me know if you want to stop okay? I want to make sure that you feel good," he started.

I flushed at his words. He definitely made me feel good.

"Okay. So what is your name? I forgot to ask that?" I said. I felt a bit odd being taken by a man whose name I didn't even know.

"Tristan."

"I'm Farah," I replied.

"Well, Farah, I'm going to take you. And I'm going to make you happy and make you feel really good," he said.

I loved the way he sounded, and soon he was hovering and kissing my body. He started to move down, lightly tugging at my dress and pulling it off. He started to lightly flick his tongue around the nipples. I gasped, for it felt even better than it had ever felt before. It was heavenly, and I know that he was the one who made me feel this good. He knew how to make me feel real pleasure, and I definitely loved that.

He started to pull off my panties, quickly getting to the part that he really wanted to get at. I wanted him to make me feel good, and despite the fact that I was a bit nervous, I did feel good about it. He started to pull down his pants, pulling his cock out and making me moan a little bit.

He then started to push himself in, starting off slowly but then getting harder and harder as time went on. This was different from when he fucked me in the butt, for this felt good. My body loved the way his cock felt inside of me, and I felt like my pussy wanted to continue to feel this way. It was amazing, and in a way, it was super wanton to me. It didn't feel like the other sex that I had felt in the past, but this one was even better than before.

He started to push even deeper into me, and his giant cock filled me up. It was definitely deeper than I had ever felt a man before. He groaned, and soon his fingers were tracing against my back as he pushed himself into me. I could feel the nails digging in, and I liked the feeling a whole lot.

As we continued to thrust against each other, I felt a haze that I had never felt before. It was a nice haze, one that felt amazing but also felt a bit odd. I didn't know if it was okay, but I definitely gave into it. I know that I was going to come soon, and after a few more thrusts, he groaned. I know that I was about to come too, and with one more thrust, I felt my pussy walls tighten up.

I let out a scream of pleasure as I felt my pussy engulf him in pleasure as I moaned, coming hard against him. He gasped as well, and then I felt his release start to come out of him and enter me. After we finished up, he pulled out and we lay on the bed.

"Well, that was fun," he remarked.

"It was. Maybe we can do it again," I replied.

He smiled. "Well, if you really want to. I'm working to be the alpha, and with sex like that I would love to have you as a mistress to me," he said.

I smiled and curled up against him, trying to find out more about this. I definitely liked the idea for some reason. Maybe it was because the guys around here were boring as shit. I didn't really know though, but I also didn't really care. After a little bit, I started to doze off, not really thinking of anything else besides the whole wolf thing and how nice this bed felt.

It was a nice sleep until about an hour later when I heard a knock on the door. Tristan got up, looking around the place to find out where the sound was coming from. The person knocked again, and this time there was a voice.

"Tristan come out. I know you're in there."

Tristan looked at me and I could tell something was wrong. I didn't know what, but something was wrong. He looked pallid, and it scared me a little.

"He's back. He's here for me."

CHAPTER 5

THE KNOCKING CONTINUED on and I didn't know what to do. I could tell from the stony face Tristan had that this was bad, that we were going to have problems. I didn't want anything bad to happen, but I could tell immediately that this was not going to end pretty. However, I know that there was a plan underneath all of this, and when I looked over at Tristan I could tell that underneath all of the worry was determination as well.

"What are we going to do?" I asked. I didn't know what else to say, and judging from the way he looked, I knew that this wasn't going to be easy at all. He was thinking, and after a minute he spoke.

"Let's wait a minute. I think I know who they are, and if they are who I think they are, we need to get the hell out of here fast," Tristan replied.

I started to feel a bit fearful. I didn't want to get hurt, but I know that this wasn't going to be a walk in the park either. There was a small window, but I don't' know if we were going to be able to leave. I looked at Tristan who was thinking about something. After about three minutes the knocking stopped and we thought that it was over. However, the knocking continued again, this time with two hands and a lot louder. They weren't stopping, and I know that I was going to be trapped.

"Open up Tristan, we know that you're in there," 'the voice said in a very gruff manner. I got scared, and I wondered what to do next. He seemed so calm and composed, but I could tell that on the inside, he was freaking the fuck out. I had to help him. I lightly grabbed his hand and looked at him, worry present in my eyes as I stared at him.

"What is going on?" I asked seriously. I could tell that it was getting to him because he lightly pushed away. I looked at him with shock on my face, but after a moment or so he started to speak.

"I need to save you. Those guys are after both of us. We have to get out here," he explained.

"But why?"

"Because you're the one that they all want. They're trying to take you as one of their own. That is a rival wolf pack outside, and I know that they mean business. The sooner we get out of here, the sooner shit stops hitting the fan and we can regroup," he explained.

I looked at him with a small look of worry. I was still awkward about trusting Tristan, but I knew that he was a person to trust.

"Plus, if we don't cooperate, they'll kill you, and I don't' want you to go like that," he explained.

I could tell from the way he looked that he wasn't fucking with me, and when I heard that they wanted me dead that was my cue to get the fuck out of there. We started to hastily get dressed, both of us still in a slight stupor from the events before. Once we were both dressed we started to walk up to the door. The booming sound of the party was still going on, but we had to muffle their screams when they came at us. I started to open the door on Tristan's cue, and when I did the wolves started to come at us.

They were real wolves too. This wasn't something out of a goddamn story book or something. This was the real thing, and I think that was the scariest thing of it all. I wasn't too freaked out over the fact that they were getting close, for whenever they did Tristan punched and kicked them, causing them to howl and whimper as they were sent flying around. It was crazy, and the whole thing seemed like a bit. I couldn't believe it, and I knew that after a while things would settle out.

There was a whole lot of fighting between him and the wolves, but soon there was no more sound from them. I don't know if he killed them or what, but I knew right then and there that they weren't going to fuck with us again. He looked at me and grabbed my hand, and I followed him out in a very surreptitious manner. We didn't want to attract attention to ourselves unless we were forced to. That was the only time.

The party was still insane at this time. There were girls doing body shots off of each other, guys going crazy about it, and there was just a whole lot of commotion going on. I couldn't believe that people were this ignorant of the fact that there was a fucking werewolf here and he was walking right out the door. Of course, we did look human so they probably just thought that we were some losers who didn't' want to stay here for hours. Which was the truth kind of, I didn't want to stay in a place where there were crazy wolves who wanted to eat at me. That wasn't my idea of fun.

After running out of there we got to his car, and even

though I was a bit scared I hopped in. At this point I didn't give a rat's ass if I was going to my death, I just wanted to be with him and away from the crazy shit that was going on. He started the car and started to drive off, but instead of going to the city or towards where my house was, we went to the forest. I wanted to ask where we were going, but at the same time, I was a bit nervous too. I didn't know if it would offend him or not if I ventured to ask something like that.

After a bit of grappling, I decided to. I know that deep down he would answer my questions. Plus, he seemed nice, and I know that he didn't have any bad intentions at all.

"Where are we going?" I asked.

"To the pack. I'm taking you there for safety," he replied.

I wondered what that meant, but after a while, I know that I would soon find out. The drive was pretty short, and soon we were in the middle of the large forest by the city. It was pretty big, and I'd been in there many times before, but we were going to a part that I had never even heard of. I know why now, though.

When we get to the place where the pack was, I looked around. There were some cars here, but at the same time, it looked so barren and odd. I didn't know if it was a bad thing or a good thing to have such a barren place for the wolf pack. I don't think it would've been easy for food or anything. Even though I had my thoughts on it, I decided to just wait and see what I was walking into.

When we got to the edge I looked at Tristan. He wasn't in the full wolf shape, but his claws were showing and his teeth were present. They were big and sharp, and I know that he was trying to transform a little bit. I looked at him with worry present on my face. Was I supposed to transform?

As if reading my mind, he shook his head, using me not to do anything. "You're new. They just want to make sure that it's me and not one of the rivals. I'll change back later on," he said.

I nodded and watched as he started to look a bit harried. It was kind of cool to see after a bit, and even though I was scared I could get used to this. We walked over to where the small fire was, and there were some wolf-like people sitting around the fire pit. One of them looked up at Tristan and smiled, and he immediately got up and walk toward her.

"Ah, if it isn't' the other man trying to take my spot," the man said. He had a grin on his face that immediately spoke of something bad, and I could tell from the way that Tristan looked he was uncomfortable in the mere presence of him. His canine teeth started to get a bit bigger and thicker, a sign that he was annoyed and pissed.

"Yes, it is me. Why, do you think I wasn't going to come back?"

"Well, I heard that there was an attack at the party you were going to, and I know that you are with you. But I also know that you're not some wolf who has only been a wolf for some time. You were one of the originals," the man said.

I looked over at him and immediately my eyes froze and my whole body felt stiff. He was about the same size as Tristan, and he had sandy blonde hair. He was like the exact opposite of Tristan, but he was also very interesting. He definitely looked hot, to say the least, and I could tell from the defined muscles that he wasn't' one that would be taken down easily. However, I was also entranced by his eyes, which were a beautiful green pair. They were in stark contrast to Tristan, who had a beautiful set of blue eyes. They looked so similar yet so different, but they both had the same effect on me. I could also see the hint of abs underneath the fur, and even though he was in the partial wolf shape, he was still really sexy and I thought he looked divine. They were so perfect, but I already knew that I was going to have issues with choosing one or the other.

They walked over to me, and I could see the fuming glance in Tristan's face. He didn't' like this man one bit. The other man had a very smug look on his face, almost like he liked to see Tristan like that. Maybe these two were brothers and they both wanted me? That could be the case, but I'm not too sure about it.

After a moment the mysterious man extended his hand and looked at me with twinkling eyes. He didn't have to say a damn thing to me and already I was mesmerized by this man's looks.

"Hello there. I'm Thomas. You must be the new fledging," he said.

I stood there agape for a little bit, trying to find the right words to say to him. I guess that's what they called me, but I saw myself as more of a person who was thrown into this mess than a person who actually knew what the fuck she was doing.

"Hi. I'm Farah. Nice to meet you."

"I take it you already met the ditto Tristan?" he cooed.

I couldn't help but giggle a little bit, but looking over at Tristan I could see him glowering. If this wasn't envy, then I didn't know what it was, and already I was growing a bit nervous.

"Yeah. He actually helped explain a lot of things to me. Plus, he's a really nice guy," I replied. I tried to at least butter him up a little bit so he wasn't too pissed at me.

However, I could see him glowering at both of us now. This was going to be awkward.

I could tell from the looks on their faces that they both wanted me, yet I could also see the intense jealousy in their faces as well. This was going to be insanely awkward, and I know that it was going to be really hard to stay here. I had to get away. Even though it was really nice of Tristan to help me out, I had to get away before things turned even crazier than before.

"So... now that we've met can I leave now? I mean I have to go back to school tomorrow. I was just out and stuff," I said. That was a lie. I didn't have classes on Saturday thank god, but I didn't know what else to say. I had to get out of there, and I know that the atmosphere was going to get even worse if I stuck around.

"Oh, nonsense, you should stick around here. Have some dinner with us. I swear, we don't bite. Hard," Thomas said. He started to roar with laughter and a couple of the other wolves that were around the fringe started to laugh as well. Tristan was already sick of their shit and he was getting angry. I didn't know what to do. However, I also saw that despite the fact that Tristan was pissed at me, he was definitely still interested in me. The way his face had a small flush when he looked at me was a sheer sign of it, and I thought it was both adorable and mysterious.

"Are you sure? I don't want to intrude or anything," I asked. I didn't want to seem rude, but I also didn't want to stay in this place for too long. It might make things even worse than they are now. Plus, judging from the way these two have been at it, I know that they are definitely not going to be nice the entire time. I could already see the anger in Tristan's face, and I know that if I ignore Thomas and leave him alone that he was going to get pissed at me as well.

There was no way that I could win, so I just had to deal with things the best way that I can.

"Not a problem at all. There is always room for a beautiful girl like you. And I assure you, I bet it will be a great meal," Thomas said.

Tristan lightly punched him in the gut, earning a pained groan from him. I laughed a little bit. They did act like boys even when they were trying to impress a lady. I couldn't help but like them.

"Sure, why not? It's not like I can leave right now. I have no clue where the hell I am," I replied.

They smiled and led me over to where the dining area was. I already felt a bit nervous about this, but at the same time, I was excited. I wanted to see what was next for me, and I know that something interesting and juicy was bound to come up.

CHAPTER 6

WHEN I GOT over to the dining area there were already people there. The other area that we were in was apparently the meeting area, and that was where both public and private meetings were held. This all seemed so damn surreal, but where I was sitting with a bunch of wolves and working with them like it was something out of Tarzan or something. Except with gorillas.

I sat there embarrassed as the people looked over me. I could tell that they were going to ask me a slew of questions, and I already could feel the nervousness starting to bubble over me. I was never good with this shit, and I know that with this it was going to be even worse.

I had a bad habit when it came to public speaking, and that was the fact that I started to sweat profusely. I didn't mean to do that, but I know that was the natural reaction. It was so unsexy, and I tried to make sure that it didn't happen in front of big meetings with my family. I used to tell myself that if I did that I would ruin the family image forever. Of course, now that I had already did that I could tell that it was the least of my worries right now. I had to figure out the best way to deal with this, and it wasn't going to be easy. That's for sure.

The first question that came out of someone's mouth was from one of the older people in the pack. I was surprised at their appearance, but they were sitting there with a keen look on their face and wondering who I was. I immediately grew nervous at the way they stared at me, but I know that I had to keep calm.

"So Farah, are you really a wolf?" the man asked.

"I am. I recently turned. Thanks to one of the guys that took me there and led me over to the wolf," I replied. I still didn't know for sure who that was, but it was certainly a mystery. It seemed like there was a lot of hearsay on that sort of thing, and I didn't know who to believe anymore.

"Well, that's good. Have you done it yet?"

"No. I almost had to earlier but then it would've attracted attention. So I didn't," I said in a confident manner. I had to prove to myself that I could actually do that, and I know that it wouldn't have been easy at all. I already know that this was going to be hard, but I had to stay strong.

"Ahh. Tell us about your life. What did you do before you came to the pack?" the man asked. It seemed like he was one of the leaders, and it was apparent that I did have to answer his questions despite how much embarrassment it might cause.

"Well, I was just a normal college girl before this. I worked hard at my studies, and I still do."

"Really? What about your family? Are they doing well? Do they know about your turning?"

"Not yet. I mean, I don't know how to really tell them that their daughter is now a wolf. You catch my drift?" I asked calmly. I didn't know how to be calm about this, but I know that it would just get worse and worse if they saw my fear. It was like dealing with an animal. If they saw your fear you were dead, and I had to keep calm.

"Ahh. So are they well off?"

I blushed at that. My dad was one of the richest men around, and I couldn't help but blush at the fact that he would immediately be recognized if I name-dropped him.

"Well, they do good for what they have. I know that they did have enough for me to go to college," I replied.

"That's nice of them to help you out."

The next couple of questions were from other mates. They were the normal things you would ask a stranger. What they liked to do, where they were from, how their family was, and if their favorite color was blue or not. I answered all of those things in a very hasty but very explicit manner. I already felt like I was going to explode with embarrassment. The dinner needed to end fast, and this dinner of roasted rabbit was going down way better than I thought it would.

Just as I thought I had answered every question in the damn book, there was one that popped up, and already I started blushing just hearing the words that were uttered.

"What about the mating thing? I heard that you were already one of the planned mates for one of the men. Have you thought any more about that?" the elder asked.

I started to flush crimson as I looked over at both Tristan and Thomas. They were looking at me with keen eyes, and I could tell that they were enjoying this. They wanted to see me suffer like this, and they certainly got their wish.

"Well, I haven't really. I don't know a whole lot about it already, so I'm not even thinking about that yet," I said.

That was the best response I could give them, and the elder seemed to like it. I don't know if it was because he liked seeing me squirm like that or what, but once that was asked the interrogation was over.

"Very well then. I guess that's all I have to ask. But I think you should start to take the mating thing a bit more seriously. We do want you to stick around, but that's the main condition," he said.

I had no clue what I wanted, and already I was starting to flush hard again. Thankfully the dinner was over and the rest of the wolves started to clear out. I saw Tristan leave with a growl on his face and a look of annoyance present in his eyes. He was pissed and jealous about something, but what it was even I didn't know. I felt awkward talking to him at this point, so I thought maybe I should sit by the meeting area and think about a few things. The fire was still going and it was pretty chilly. However, just as I was about to get up, Thomas looked at me with a smile on his face. It wasn't one of malice or anything, but one that meant that he genuinely wanted to talk to me.

"Say, do you want to come back to my area? I have a small den over on the eastern side, and I think we need to have a little chat. Especially since there is some unfinished business between us," he asked.

I grew nervous just hearing those words. I didn't' know what the fuck I did wrong, but I could feel my face flushing as I thought of it. I didn't want to piss him off, and I felt like that was what I did. However, he grabbed my hand and led me down to his den.

When we got there, he opened the small curtain that guarded and shrouded the area and walked in. We walked about fifty feet in before I saw the small bedding area along with a small gas lamp. It was kind of nice and cozy, and I could feel the heat rising on my face. This was like something out of one of those crappy romance movies where the girl sits with a guy and he admits that he loves her and she loves him. However, that's not how I felt with this guy. In fact, I felt completely exposed and nervous. I didn't know this man for shit, and I felt completely nervous around him.

"What's wrong? Cat got your tongue?" he asked. The silence broke, and I tried to think of what to say next.

"Well... it's not that. It's something else altogether, though," I replied.

"What is it?"

I tried to get my thoughts straight around me, but already I was flushing. It was so hard to talk about this type of thing with a guy I barely met. All I know was that I liked him, and I liked Tristan, but I didn't know whom to choose. I was stuck between two beautiful men, and it was the hardest feeling imaginable.

"Well, I dunno. I just feel weird that I don't really know you, but I do want to. But there is the other factor of Tristan and he already looked like he was going to bite my head off and mutilate yours," I replied.

"Well, I'm Thomas. I'm one of the future leaders of the pack. So is Tristan. Basically, we're both in the running for that position. However, I have the upper hand because I have the power. I have parents that have power, and they gave that power to me. So I do have a bit of an unfair advantage, but he still continues on going along. However, I know that things have gotten worse between both of us because of the mate thing. But don't worry about him. He's not going to bother you. I'm here now, so only think about that," he cooed.

I looked at him and my body started to feel hot. I wanted him. I craved him for some weird fucking reason. Hell, I didn't even know him. But I just wanted him, and I knew that the want was only getting worse and worse. I could feel the aching between my legs, and I wanted him to satisfy me.

But there was the part of me that was worried that if I did these things with Tristan it would be like committing adultery. Sure, I wasn't' attached to him or to anyone else, but it still was a bit unsettling in my mind. I didn't like the way that it rested, but what could I do? I wanted both of them, but I could only have one.

"But—"

He pushed his hand to my lips, lightly silencing me with the gesture. It felt so nice and soft, and already I felt like my mind was lost in the abyss of his beautiful air around him. I wanted him so badly, and I know that the want was only going to get worse as time went on.

"Don't worry about Tristan, my dear. You have me instead, and I'll make sure that you feel damn good," he replied.

Before I could say anything he pulled me into his lap, earning a small yelp from me. I wasn't annoyed and I didn't want to leave, but I was embarrassed by all of the touching. I had never been touched so much by him, and the fact that he was lightly running his hands all over my body made me want him even more. It was like an avid craving, and already I wanted my desires to be satisfied by him.

He started to move his lips right over the shell of my ear, licking it and causing a small mewl to escape me. It was the most wanton sound ever, but Thomas got a kick out of it. He started to do it more, and my moans came out in small gasps. Already I could feel the heat off myself pooling all up inside of me, and I know that it was only getting worse. I wanted him, craved him, and I know that it was only a matter of time before he did the dirtiest things to me. There was no way I was going to stop him, though, since I wanted him to. I wanted him to take me, and I wanted him to use me and have his way with me.

He started to lightly press his lips right up against my ear, nibbling it a little bit while he sucked on the earlobe. I moaned, my back arching in pleasure as he did this. He continued to lightly nibble on it, and I moaned with wanton pleasure as he did this. It felt amazing, and already I could feel the haze on my body start to cloud over me and make me feel a bit dizzy.

He started to move his body so that he could position me so that our faces were against each other. He lightly traced his hand against the jawline of my face, and I flushed at the feeling. He then started to move his tongue from the shell of my ear all the way down to the edge of my lip, lightly touching the side of it. I moaned, my body going crazy with lust as he did this. It felt so good, and I wanted him to do even more for me.

He did that again, teasing me a few times before he pushed his lips on mine, kissing me hard and passionately. This was different than when Tristan kissed me. This one was filled with an animalistic passion. Sure, he was still in the half wolf form, but it was different than just that. This felt so much rawer and I liked it a whole lot. I wanted to be treated like a dirty woman, and this man was going to make me do that.

He started to push his body on top of mine, pushing me onto the little bed that he had. Our mouths did not move off of each other as he did that, and I still felt his tongue linger deep into my oral cavern. It was an amazing feeling, and the way he moved his tongue all over me made me want him even more than I did before. He started to lightly massage his tongue over mine, causing me to moan in pleasure as he did that. He gripped my hips, pulling me up and deepening the kiss even harder than he did before. It was a fit of passion that I had never felt before, and already I was starting to go crazy with lust by the sheer feeling of it.

He started to pull off the dress that I was wearing. It was different than when Tristan did this. This one was almost like he was ripping my clothes off, and it almost hurt a little bit had I not been drunk with pleasure and want. He started to lightly nibble at my neck, biting on it and causing me to moan. It felt good, but it also hurt a little bit. I didn't' feel the drawing of blood, but I didn't know anymore. I was so overcome with lust and pleasure that I didn't' really care either. If he bit me then I was going to go crazy and let him continue. I wanted him to do that, and he seemed to grant my wish.

He continued to do this to me until he got to where my breasts were. They were already swelling and my nipples were pink with desire. I could feel them hardening as he started to move his lips closer to them, and soon he hovered over them. He started to lightly suck on one, putting his two fingers in between the other one and playing with them. The feeling of pleasure continued to course through me and already I felt like I was on a high that I wasn't going to come down from. I also didn't' want to come down from it, and he knew that as well.

He continued to ravish my body, making me moan in pleasure at the feeling that he gave me. The sucking was nice, but when he lightly grazed his teeth against it, that's when I went crazy. I had never imagined myself to be the one who was into pain, but goddamn it felt good. I wanted more from him, and he could immediately tell that I was horny for more.

He started to pull away, and I wondered what he was going to do to me. Instead, he went over to the little side table, he had and pulled out a small ribbon along with a rag. He pushed the rag into my mouth and bound my arms before I could say anything, and even though I was a bit nervous and I gasped at the feeling, I also kind of liked it. I was naked, bound, and gagged by this man, and I craved more from him.

"There you go. Now that you're all quiet I can give you the real pleasure that you want," he said. He started to lick his lips and I could see from the lustful gaze in his eyes that he was ready to have some fun.

He started to lick down my body, trailing kisses with his tongue. It felt a little bit rougher than before, but I didn't mind it at all. He started to move down to where my pussy was, and I was already soaked with pleasure. He pushed his tongue right up against the clit, causing me to moan. He licked and sucked on it while his hands started to push in and out of my pussy, and already I felt like I was on my edge. My moans came out in little spurts, and Thomas loved the way that I sounded, apparently, it was really hot, and he continued his onslaught on my body with both his mouth and his tongue against my hungry pussy,

I didn't know the first time I climaxed. I climaxed about three times just by him doing that. Each orgasm was more powerful than the last one, and I could feel my breathing start to grow even raspier than before. I loved it, and he definitely loved seeing my reaction as well.

He started to pull away, and even though I was a bit sad that he was done he had another thing coming. He started to pull down his pants, revealing his large cock. It was about ten inches long, and I could see the heat coming from it. It was already slick with precum, and I could see that his tip was already red and ready for me.

He pushed himself on top of me and spread my legs,

allowing himself to come into my body. I was a bit nervous to do it with a guy like him, but at the same time, I felt the nerves start to get overcome with pleasure and lust. He started to push himself harder into me, causing me to almost scream out. It was like he was completely filling me up. This was the biggest cock that I've ever had in my body, and I loved how it felt.

He started to wait for a second while my body got used to the feeling. I could feel my pussy growing numb from the sheer largeness of him. But I had to take him, and soon he started to move up and down against me. His cock filled me up, and whenever he pulled out it almost felt empty. However, when he pushed himself back in again, it was like a surge of pleasure coursed through me and a moan escaped my lips. He continued to do that harder and harder, and already I felt like I was at my limit. There was no way I could continue on. Of course, I didn't know if he was anywhere close yet.

Thankfully, I could tell that he was getting very close. After a couple more thrusts he screamed out, and I felt his cum shoot out of his cock and start to fill me up. It was an amazing feeling, and I already felt like my body was high on the lust that I felt. I know that my orgasm was looming right over me, and after one last thrust, I lost it.

I let out a loud scream, my body contorting in pleasure as I let out my release. I gasped at the way it felt, and the fact that my body was able to take his giant cock was something in it itself. It was definitely amazing, and that orgasm was by far the best and most powerful one I had ever had.

After he finished up, he pulled out, his cum still all over my pussy. He had a huge load, and I could tell that it was going to take a lot to clean this up. After I cleaned it, I sat next to him and smiled.

"So how did you like that? I told you I was an animal in bed," he said.

"Well, it was certainly... nice," I replied. I didn't know what to say exactly to him, but I did like the way I was treated. However, there was something looming over me that made me worry, a feeling that I was doing the wrong thing. I wanted both of them, but I didn't know what to do. As I sat there with him a couple of burning questions started to fill my head. I wanted to sleep, but I didn't know if I could just yet.

Who do I choose? Was this the right thing?

CHAPTER 7

AS I THOUGHT of those things, I started to drift off. I still didn't know who I wanted just yet, but at the same time, I didn't want to know what to think next. I did want them both, and I was conflicted by the feeling that it gave me. Who should I choose? Was it bad to want them both?

I'd never had been in a relationship where I got to have two guys. That just seemed so wrong. However, I know they did that a lot in Europe and such, and maybe it would be okay here. But at the same time, I could see my parents flipping their shit when it came to that sort of thing. They'll think I was fucking every guy in town, which in some ways wasn't far from the truth when it came to my past. I was a flit, what can I say?

I didn't know what to do, though, and that kept me up. I started to cuddle up to Thomas though and fall asleep in his arms. He was very warm, and he definitely felt really nice around my body. It was almost like his wolf self was holding me, but I didn't' feel any fur or hair besides the ones that I had before. I know that it must have just been the way I was sitting, but damn this was really relaxing. I know that if I wanted to, I could certainly fall asleep like this.

The night started to wear on and I was soon conked out. The sleep didn't last forever though, because about an hour later I was woken up with a loud bang and some screaming. Immediately, Thomas got up, putting his pants on and walking up to where the noise was. When he walked outside, he immediately turned back to me, a pained expression on his face.

"We have to get out of here!" he screamed at me.

I know that he didn't mean to, but it was a bit touchy. I was a bit scared about all of this, so I managed to simply nod. I didn't know what was going on, but I simply put my clothes back on and started to follow suit. There was no way in hell I was getting caught out there or alone in here with whatever the hell was going on out there. Something was definitely going on, but I had no idea what it was until it was too late.

I started to trudge outside, the sleep that I didn't get starting to catch up to me. I felt super drowsy from the feeling of sex plus the fact that I hadn't slept at all period for a while. However, when I got out there I immediately started to wake up. It was like something out of an apocalyptic movie, and I know that this wasn't good at all.

There was fire everywhere, and the main fire pit was actually not burning. Something else did this. I could hear the sounds of stabbing and gunshots along with the sounds of something being gorged. I didn't know what was going on. However, before I could ask Thomas pulled me over to the side. He started to get a look at them and immediately blanched when he saw who it was.

"Oh shit," he said.

I looked at him with a curious glance, trying to figure

out what to say. However, after a moment or so I finally spoke. "What's going on?" I asked. I felt so stupid, but I didn't know what else to say. I felt very out of the loop, and this wasn't something to be at a time like this.

"We're being attacked by a rival pack. We have to get out of here before it's too late!" he said aloud.

I nodded and started to run with him, and soon we met up with the elder and Tristan. Tristan was huffing and puffing and I could tell that he hadn't slept a whole lot either. He looked at me and scowled, and I could tell that he's pissed. He probably doesn't even know about the whole sex thing, but can tell just by looking at my face.

"What the hell are you doing?" he asked.

"Me? I was wondering the same about you. Who could be attacking us? Do you think it's time?"

"Can't be Thomas, we paid off our dues to them last week. We have the treaty in effect, but obviously either someone fucked it up and decided to start shit, or there's a spy around here somewhere," Tristan replied. He looked right over at Thomas, who was waving his arms.

"Why are you blaming me? You know that I may come from royal blood, but I'm not a traitor," he said.

"Well, I'll believe it when I see it," Tristan said bluntly. He turned to me with a pissed expression.

"We'll talk about the rest later. Right now we have to get the fuck out of here," Tristan said to me. The three of us nodded and started to run away from the camp. However, one of them saw us and started to barrel over to us. Immediately we started to pick it up, all three of us wondering if we could really outrun this damn thing.

'Shit. What do we do?" Tristan asked.

"Well, we're going to have to run and get out of here. Let's head over to an ally pack. We can lay low there and try to formulate a strategy and try to figure out who the fuck is trying to hurt us," Thomas replied.

I nodded, my body starting to grow tired. I don't' know why I felt like this. Maybe I was still weak from earlier. Yet I had sex with Tristan and I was able to run fine. Maybe it was something else altogether. I wasn't going to try to think about it and I was just going to run.

We continued to run for about half a mile, but they were still chasing us. I couldn't go on much longer and i started to slow down. I felt Tristan grab my hand and pull me, his body dragging as well.

"Come on Farah, we have to hurry," he said.

I nodded and started to move even faster, trying to go as quick as I could. After a few more steps though I heard a scream and turned around.

Tristan was on the ground and I could see that his foot was twisted on a branch. I looked at Thomas, who was standing in place for a second.

"Leave him. We have to run," he said.

I thought about what I was doing, but I know that this was the right thing to do. I shook my head and headed back, trying to undo Tristan's foot from the brambles of the plant. He looked at me with a shocked expression on his face. I don't think he'd ever been saved like this before. It was probably something new to him.

"Why did you come back?" he asked.

"Because I want to help you out. You're not going to get caught and leave me to be free," I replied. I had no clue what I was doing. Was I trying to assert my love or desire for him or something? Was I just being a goddamn idiot? I felt like it was more of the latter, but a part of me did feel like the knight in shining armor helping out the man. Of course, he was far from being a princess.

However, just as I was about to pull him up we got surrounded. There were ten wolves all around us, and they all had their teeth bared. One of them started to speak.

"You're no match for us. Surrender now," he said.

Tristan wanted to go after him, but I place my hand on his shoulder. He was hurt, and I could tell that he was tired. There was no way we could win, so he simply put his hands up and just walked with them.

They started to lead us somewhere, to a sort of little cart or something. We were stuffed in there together and taken away, and the last thing I remember seeing was Thomas' shocked expression followed by a glowering grin.

"What the—" I said aloud.

However, just as I looked over it was gone, and the only thing that was there before started to fade into the night until the pitch blackness was the only thing that remained.

Tristan and I were quiet for the entire ride, both of us unsure of what to do next. I wanted to say something, but I held my tongue. I didn't want to cause any more issues between us.

The cart took us down a road and then down a windy path. That was the last thing I remembered feeling. After that I dozed off into the slumber that I was in, trying to think of what was in store for us next.

CHAPTER 8

I STILL DIDN'T KNOW where I was. I was scared, and I could feel my body shaking with worry as I sat there. It was very scary in here, but I didn't know what to do. I was trapped, and in this small and dank space where here I was going to end up being for the rest of my life. Of course, that's what I thought.

When I woke up after I got knocked out I found out I was here. I was in the same cell as Tristan, and we were both in here and not able to escape. We still had our clothes, but our bodies both had bruises and neither of us knew where they came from. It was a tad scary, but I didn't know what to do about it. It was like there was something missing, and neither of us knew what was going on.

I tried to keep calm, but as I thought about it my eyes started to water a little bit. I felt scared and trapped, and there was no way in hell I was getting out of here soon. I had to leave, for the sake of my own body and of Tristan's.

I could tell each day that Tristan was starting to grow weaker. I believe we sat in that cell for about five days before he really opened up to me, and even then he was still a bit nervous, to say the least. I would be too if I had to figure out how to get myself out of here before it was too late. I sat in the corner of my own cell, thinking about this entire thing. It was a bit nerve-wracking, but I had to stay strong for everyone. There was no way I was going to attempt to show any emotion unless if it was too late.

After the third day, though, I started to crack. Tears started to come to my eyes for about two days, and I wanted to just die. There was no way I was going to go through with this, and I know that I had to think of something. I felt so lost and alone, yet I didn't know what to do or what to think.

I continued to cry for the next couple of days after that. It had been about seven days, at this point. The guards came by once in a while to laugh at us and give us food, saying we were goddamn heretics or something. What the hell that meant, even I didn't know. It was like they were saying we did something wrong when I didn't know what in the world was going on in the first place.

The first time Tristan spoke to me was very softly. I could tell that he was broken, and the way that he spoke was utterly pathetic to me. I wanted to hold him in my arms, to caress him, and to make him feel better. I don't know why I even though that way about him so much recently, but that was what I wanted and I know that it was going to be the way that I felt for a long time.

"So... what do we do now?" he asked.

I looked at him, tears welling up in my eyes. I didn't know what to do next. And I felt completely lost just thinking about it. I had to do something, and even if that something was small I know that it would mean the world to him.

"We have to get out of here. I don't know how, but we will," I replied. I started to get up when his hand weakly extended out, grabbing mine and pulling me closer. I lightly squeaked when I felt his hand cover mine, and soon I was on his lap. We looked at each other both of us blushing furiously at the way we looked. After a minute or so he finally spoke, and I was still awkward about this whole thing.

"Listen, Farah, there's something that I want to say. I don't know what, but I know that I have to say this to you or else I'm going to have a heavy heart and I don't know if we'll make it out of here," he admitted.

I thought he was fucking joking when he said that, but as I looked at him I could tell that the truth was there. He was scared, and I know that it was only going to get worse from here.

"What do you mean?"

"What I mean is there is something that I've meant to tell you for a very long time, but I didn't know how to bring it up. Since we're in this shitty situation now, though, I think now is the best time to really say how I feel," he replied.

I wondered what he meant, but before I could ask he pressed his lips to mine, lightly kissing them softly. I kissed them back, my body confused with worry about what the hell was going on. We stayed like that for a bit before he pulled away, looking at me with a very embarrassed gaze on his face.

"Well... the truth of the matter is, I love you, Farah. I thought it was maybe just the stupid mating crap, but this is something more. I love you, and I know that's how I feel about you," he admitted.

I didn't know what to say. This was beyond my imagination, and I couldn't believe that he was admitting something like this to me. I liked it a lot, but at the same time, I was very nervous. I didn't know how to feel about something like this, and even though I wanted to say yes I was still awkward about it.

"Do you really love me?" I asked. I wanted to make sure that the love was real. I've been in relationships and been in love before, but that was all just a lie in order to get me to think about them even more and to stay in the relationship. This seemed real though, and as I looked at him I knew that it was.

"Yes, it is Farah. I love you so much," he replied.

I smiled, and soon my lips were pressed to his once again. This kiss was way more impassioned this time, and our tongues started to do a fiery dance with each other. We were both moaning and groaning, and I loved the way that it felt. It was so damn amazing, and I know that it was way too good to be true.

After a moment we both pulled away, looking at each other and trying to catch our breaths. That was the first kiss we had after we both admitted our feelings, and I know that this was the right thing to do.

"I love you too Tristan. I tried to hide it before, but at the same time, I knew that it was wrong. I love you so damn much, and I know that this was definitely the right thing in my mind," I replied.

He smiled, and in response he pressed his lips to me once again, both of us making out in a dance of fiery passion. It was amazing, and already I was moaning with lust and pleasure. He was groaning as well as our tongues started to mingle and move with each other. He lightly massaged his tongue against mine, and I moaned wantonly as he continued to do that. It was by far the best feeling ever, and I know that nothing was ever going to top this. I loved the way that he made out, for he was really good at it.

He started to push me up against the wall, and soon he

started to hike my dress up. I lightly gasped as I felt the cold floor against my bare behind. I hadn't changed clothes in days, and I still had the clothes that I had when I was kidnapped. It didn't feel good at all, to say the least, but I know that I really didn't have a say in what to wear at this point.

He continued to make out with me while he moved his hand against my bare ass, cupping it and making me moan. He started to move to another area, and soon his hand was right by my other hole. He was starting to touch the edge of my anus, and I immediately gasped.

"W-what are you doing?" I asked.

"Have you ever done anal before?" he asked.

I thought about it, and I actually hadn't. That was something that I wanted to do a while back, but I never found the right guy to do it with. This sounded like fun though, and it would be different from the normal vaginal fucking that I was used to.

I hadn't... but I'm willing to try," I replied. I was still a bit shaky about all of that, but Tristan simply smiled at me as he looked at my body.

"Don't worry babe, I'll take good care of you and help stretch you out before I go in," he said.

Even though the words sounded lewd, I was already getting turned on by that. I wanted him to do this, and I could tell that he wanted to do this as well.

He pushed me up against the wall so that my butt was facing him, ND while he started to finger my pussy I could feel his hands right by my mouth. I looked at him with wonder and he smiled at me.

"Just suck on them," he instructed.

I had never done anything like this before, so I sucked on them just like he said. I made them really slimy, and once I did that he started to push his hand under my thong and slide it down. He moved the finger right by my entrance, tickling it before he went in.

The feeling when it went in was better than anything I had ever felt before. It was by far the best pleasure I had ever received, and it was so nice. He started to lightly prod at the edge of it, writing a minute or so before he started to push himself inside of me. I could feel him inside my walls, and already I was moaning and going crazy with lust. It was so damn good, and he loved the reaction that he got out of me. I could tell that he hadn't done something like this in a very long time, and the results that he was getting were the best things about it.

He started to push it in deeper, and I actually felt wetter down there. He started to finger my pussy while his other hand played with my ass, and already I was holding onto the wall for support. The pleasure was going through me, but I know that it was only going to get better from here. I wanted him, and he was definitely going to have a whole lot of fun with me.

After playing with me a little bit he pulled away, leaving me moaning in anticipation. I wanted him to have his way with me, and I wanted his cock right then and there. He started to undo his pants and pull them down, revealing his large and throbbing cock. It was standing completely erect, and already I could feel my mouth salivating in want and desire when I saw it.

"Damn," I said aloud.

"What? You want it?" he cooed. He started to lightly tease my entrance, and I could feel my breath hitching.

I-I do," I replied. I had to admit that the suspense was killing me and I loved the way that it felt.

He smiled and started to push his cock into my

entrance, holding my body so that I didn't move too much. The pain was almost unbearable, and already I felt like I was regretting this, yet I also knew that later on, it was going to feel good. Sure enough, once he was fully in it actually felt amazing, and the feeling that I had was replaced by the numb feeling of his cock inside of my butt.

He started to move in and out of me and I moaned at the tight feeling that he had. It was definitely different from my pussy, and it actually burned a little bit as he thrust into me. Yet at the same time, I liked it a whole lot, and I could tell that this was only the beginning of something even better than what I had thought before.

He continued to push himself in and out of me harder and harder, and I was moaning like crazy. He continued that for a little bit, and I could hear him struggling for breaths. After a few more thrusts, I heard him groan and I knew at that point it was the end. He was already going crazy for me, and I was going nuts for him as well.

When I felt him come it was a very different feeling than what I was used to. It was nice, and I liked how deep it went. While he finished up, he pushed his fingers deep into me as well, causing me to moan and finally release as well. My fingers tightened around him and I could feel my ass clench up around his hard member as I finally came, my own essence escaping my body and coating my outer vulva.

After he finished up, he pulled out of me and smiled. We were both spent, and he definitely looked happy. He pulled me into his arms and gave me a kiss, causing me to blush.

"I love you, Farah."

"I love you too Tristan," I replied.

We sat like that for a while, and then soon I got my clothes back on. At that point, the guard doors opened and what looked to be the leader of all the men came over and looked at us, a frown present on his face. He totally looked like someone pooped in his cornflakes, and he was not happy one bit when he saw us sitting there.

"You guys will be executed on the spot tomorrow. Tonight is your last."

CHAPTER 9

WHEN THE GUARD left I looked at Tristan with a shocked expression. I didn't know how to handle something like this. This was way different than anything I had ever done before, and I didn't like the way that it felt.

"What are we going to do?" I asked.

I saw the look on Tristan's face and already I knew that shit was about to hit the fan. I didn't know what to think about all of this, and it was definitely going to be a bumpy ride.

"Well, we have to form a plan first and foremost. That's the most important part of all of this," he explained.

I nodded, trying to figure out the best plan possible. There were a lot of choices. We could always go with the busting through, but that might just lead to us getting hurt. However, there was also the other factor of us trying to sneak out, but that might require a whole lot more than what it might take. There was a lot to figure in, and judging from the look on his face I could tell that Tristan was already a few steps ahead of me.

"Well, there really is no way to sneak out. I hate to say

this, but I think we might have to escape the old-fashioned way. That means that we have to go through and take them all out at once," he explained.

"But... how? I mean, sure, it might seem okay in theory, but I don't think in practice it's going to work out so well," I admitted. Not only was I a bit nervous, but I was also kind of scared shitless about what this might mean for the rest of us. Plus there was the pack to think about, and I don't even want to imagine what they were going through right now because of us.

"Well, we're going to have to take out the guard and then we're going to run. If I remember the rival's den right, I think we're in the main holding cell. That means that right outside is where the chief of the pack lives, and I know that his mate is pretty ferocious as well. This pack is bad news, and we have to get out of here before we get hurt," he instructed.

I nodded, trying to catch up with everything. There was a lot to take in, and I was scared, to say the least. I still didn't know what this was all going to mean for me, but I had to follow his lead when the timing was right.

That night, the night guard came over to give us some food, and that was the opening that we needed. We immediately jumped, the guard going crazy with fear. Immediately Tristan tore his jugular, leaving him there to die as he clawed his throat. He wasn't going to live for a long time.

After that, he grabbed my hand and we started to run. I could hear the alarm and all of the other guards coming out and going after us. Something was wrong, and I know that this was not the way things were supposed to go. I could tell immediately that Tristan was scared. However, he continued to stay strong as he ran through the whole place, and soon we were finally out. This was like the run of our lives, and I know that I was trying to move as fast as possible so I could get out of there fast.

It seemed like we were home free, at least that's how it looked like. Of course, I know that things were not going to go the way that we had planned, and sure enough they did not. When we got out we saw the head of the pack there, and when I saw who it was I let out a shrill gasp.

Right in front of us was Thomas, and he already had a woman next to him. The guy was a liar and a cheater, and I know that he just used me the entire time. I fell for the wrong man at first, and I immediately regret it the minute I saw him and the guild lurch in my stomach.

CHAPTER 10

I SAW the same look on Tristan when he saw Thomas standing there. He had a look of pure hatred on his face, and he lightly touched the top of the woman's head. He was using her, and I could tell immediately that he was not a good guy. He wanted to see me riled up, and judging from the look on his face he was getting what he wanted.

"Ahh, Farah a pleasure to see you here. You too Tristan, but I know that this will probably be the last time that we ever see each other," he cooed in a very low voice. The female wolf started to laugh with him, and they started to laugh like a bunch of hyenas. It was really annoying, but I know that he was definitely just trying to get a rise out of me. That was not going to happen right now.

As I stood there I could tell that the other wolves were all around me. They all had the same look of terror on their face as they looked at me, and already I could feel my body tensing up. They wanted to see me like this, and they surely got their wish.

I wanted to run away, but the question was where. I had no clue where to go, and already Tristan was starting to grow as nervous as I was. I had to take care of him, for I could tell from the way he was holding my hand that he was about to do something very fucking stupid. However, I didn't know how long I could hold it off before things got really bad.

"So what do you want Thomas? Why did you take us?" I asked.

He started to chuckle and the other wolves started to as well. His mate was hanging all over him, and I could tell that she was looking at me with a stony glare.

"Well simple, because I wanted to finally destroy my rival once and for all," he replied.

I wanted to figure all of this out, but Tristan beat me to the next question.

"You're not the head of the pack! Charles is!" he cried out.

Thomas started to almost bowl over with laughter at those words. I had no idea who Charles was, but I assumed that it was the head of the pack. Or at least, the head of this one. However, I soon saw Thomas start to morph into something else, something akin to an old man. He definitely looked way different.

"Well, as you can see, I still am Charles. I am a shifter as well, both as a wolf and a man and as from young to old. I can choose how old I want to be, and I can also choose if I want to be a wolf or not. That's a lot more than you can do right?" he cooed.

I could see the anger start to boil inside of Tristan's face. He was so angry at this man, and I could see his other hand grow into a fist. It was a bit scary, and I started to lightly tug away. However, he kept his hold on me as he looked at him.

"But why? Why were you spying on us? What did you think you could achieve by doing that?" he asked.

The man started to laugh and started to morph even more into the older figure that I saw before. This was like something out of the Twilight Zone or something.

"Because my friend, I like to see you squirm. I like to make sure that you're on the edge of your seat and you're worried about everything," he replied.

Tristan looked at him with a worried glance as the man started to morph into the wolf shape that he had. He was still smiling, and when I looked at him, he kind of reminded me of the Cheshire Cat when he looked like that. It was a grin of pure evil, and both of us knew that. This man was bad news, and he was only getting worse.

"But why did you spy on us? What did you have to gain?"

"Well, isn't that a simple question too Tristan? And you're supposed to be the new alpha male. Wow, I can't believe that you're so damn stupid," he replied.

"Don't fuck with me right now! What are you trying to get?" Tristan bellowed.

"It's simple really. I wanted to use the pack to take over and control everything. I had just about everything too until my comrades went full stupid and tried to burn the place down. That was supposed to happen after I was head of the pack, and once that occurred then you would be gone and I would have your entire group under my control. Of course, most of them are dead now and that would've been where they would've ended up," he replied. He started to laugh even louder and Tristan was growing even angrier.

"Shut up! You're nothing but a goddamn monster, and you need to be vanquished," he said. Tristan started to turn into a wolf himself, and I immediately grew nervous as I looked at both of them. I had only heard of them doing this once before, and when I saw it the last time it did shock me a tiny bit. Of course, this time it worried me even more, for I was on the sidelines and not able to do anything. A couple of the other wolves that Thomas had tried to attack Tristan, but he simply cut them down and they all howled in pain. He started to circle around and so did Thomas, both of them looking at each other with an intent to kill.

"This is our fight, Thomas. Leave your people out of this or I'll have to kill them all," Tristan said.

"Go ahead, I wouldn't give a damn if you did," he said. Immediately they started to run into the fight, and I was off on the sidelines. I could only watch from afar what was about to go down, but the thought of it started to make me even more scared than I had ever been before.

CHAPTER 11

I WAS off on the side, and the only thing that I could do now was hope. I felt so damn weak in this situation, but there was nothing I could do. I didn't have the power that he did, so I had to just watch from the side and hope that everything was okay in the end. I know that it would, but in my mind, I always thought of the worst beforehand.

I didn't know what was going on for the first ten minutes of the fight. It was so blurry that it looked like two alley cats going at it. The other wolves were cheering on Thomas, and I could hear the human voices as well. I had to cheer on Tristan, but I was too quiet when it came to all of them. I was going to cheer him on, but I wanted to do it my own way.

I started to put my hands together in the meditation position. I was really into that crap back in my early college days, but now I didn't' really do a whole lot with it. However, as I sat there and started to meditate and pray a little bit, I hoped that he would be okay. That was the only thing on my mind at the moment, that he would walk out of this with as few injuries as possible. I know that I would probably not get that, but it was the only thing that I could ask for at this point. I just wanted him to live more than anything and I wanted to make sure that I would get to kiss those lips once again. I wasn't religious by any means, but if it meant that he would be alive once again, I know that it would mean the world to me.

I watched the battle continue on and I was getting scared at the way things were going. They both looked really beaten up, and I hated to see how they would look at the end of this. I could see the gashes all over them, and a part of me wanted to go out there and stop, but I know that wasn't the right thing to do. This was their fight, and although I was kind of the Kewpie prize in this, I know that it was definitely not the right thing to do. I had to stay strong for both of them, for I know that Tristan would need me and I know that Thomas would need to be taught a lesson.

I could hear the howling from both parties and every time I heard a Tristan scream out all of the other wolves started to roar out. I was pretty shocked that none of them harassed me, but I bet they were waiting for Thomas to win so that they could do those things without getting in trouble. These guys were pigs, to say the least. Hell, I think some of the guys that I went to parties with had more class than these dudes. They were all hollering aloud and it was definitely not cool. I just wanted to punch them all in the face more than anything, and I definitely wanted to see them groan when I saw Tristan walk out of there unharmed and with me.

The fight continued on and I saw nothing but dark patches and blood everywhere. These two were relentless. Even though there was a lot of fighting these guys just didn't want to stop. It was like they couldn't stop doing that, and that was the scariest part of all of that. I didn't want to see either of them hurt, but if Thomas had to get hit then so be it.

At one point I heard all of them roar loudly, and I thought that it was over. However, when I finally caught a glimpse, it was worse than I thought. They were all beaten and bloody, and tufts of their hair were gone. It looked like a mess, and both of them looked like dogs who just got a bad haircut from the groomer's. It was not cool, and already I could feel my heart sinking,. But that was the least tan.

He was down on the ground and Thomas had him pinned down. They were both fighting each other at this point, and soon I saw Tristan get pushed down even more. Thomas had his paw against Tristan's throat, and I could hear the gasps coming out of him. I didn't want this to be the end. Please don't let it be the end.

Thankfully though, my prayers were answered as I saw Tristan get up and started to push him back. Thomas fell back against a tree and that's when Tristan struck. He immediately bit into his throat, tearing away at it and causing a gash that immediately spits out blood like it was a waterfall. I was shocked at all of this, but I know that it's for the best. Besides, if this saved my life I didn't care what the fuck happened. What's done is done, and I know that it was for the best and I know that I had to do this.

After he finished tearing away at his throat he got away from the body and came over to me, smiling.

"Hey, there babe. I did it. I saved you from them," he replied. I wanted to help him, and I wanted to tend to his injuries. However, just as we were about to walk away the crowd started to that they were rioting against the loss. I could even hear it in some of the people.

"You fucking bastard!"

"You'll pay for this!"

"I'll kill you!"

Those were the things uttered out of their mouths, and that's what sickened me. I hated hearing those words, but I know that they were all pissed at me. I had to get away from them, and immediately I pulled Tristan up onto my shoulder and started to run. It wasn't the smartest move, but what other choice did I have? I had to get him the fuck out of there fast.

We started to barrel out of the forest. The other wolves started to catch up, and at one point there was nothing but other wolves around us. We were trapped.

I tried to think of something, and immediately a crazy idea came to me. I started to shift myself, and for the first time, I turned into a wolf. I growled my teeth at the men and started to yell at them with the low voice that I had when I was in my wolf form.

"Get the hell away from me!" I yelled.

The other wolves started to come at me, but I struck them down with my claws into their eyes. They immediately howled over in pain as I took my claws out of their eyes. It was pathetic to see them, but I know that I had to do that. It was the only way to save Tristan. Plus, it was kind of funny how pathetic these men looked after I was done with them. It made me feel stronger in ways I never imagined myself to be strong.

I started to grab Tristan and soon we were out of that half of the forest. Tristan was already growing weak, and immediately I saw a small motel nearby. Shockingly enough, I still had my debit card on me. Even though my parents were probably going to wonder who I was with this time, I didn't give a damn. I had to save Tristan from this.

I grabbed him and brought him to a motel, laying him down on the bed. I went to the gas station to buy some first aid stuff and started to bandage him up. After a while, he started to groan and I looked at him.

"I'm... alive?" he asked aloud. I could tell that this was shocking to him, and I was perplexed that he made it myself.

"Yes, you did. I got a motel for the night. In the morning we can go back to the den," I said.

He nodded and started to fall asleep. I curled up next to him and lightly rubbed his head. He was the love of my life, and I was able to save him. And I was also able to help him through this.

CHAPTER 12

THE NEXT DAY, we made it back to the den, and immediately everyone looked at us with shocked looks on their faces. I never imagined they would be so happy to see us, but immediately we were greeted with cheers and congrats.

Soon Tristan was taken back and immediately granted the title of being the alpha wolf and I was happy for him. The rest of the pack was already cheering and excited, and I was so happy to see that he was happy. I felt a little bit awkward, however, and I could tell that he did as well.

The next few months were spent with him. I still went to class, but at night I stayed with him and the pack. After I finished college, I decided to live with the pack as a shifter. My parents didn't ask where I was, and they just assumed that I was staying with a friend. I never told them about the adventures here. They wouldn't understand them if it bit them in the ass and called itself Amanda.

After a little bit, I could tell that Tristan wanted to ask me something. He was starting to get a bit weird around me, and I know that he definitely wanted to find out something about me. I wanted to talk to him as well, and after a little bit he pulled me off to the side. I wondered what it was, but he led me to his place where he lived now. He was now the alpha, and I was just another lady in the pack. There were other girls, but he still had his eyes on me. I honestly didn't' know why.

That night, though, he pulled me to the side and looked at me with a smile. I wondered what it was, but soon he started to speak.

"So it's official. I'm the alpha now," he said.

"I know you are," I replied.

That seemed like almost old news, but from the way he looked at me, there was something else added to it that definitely made it interesting.

"Well, yeah, but there is another thing that I have to do first. I have to find a mate. And I found one. And I wanted to give her something tonight to show that I loved her," he said.

"What do you mean, I thought I was—"

Before I could say anything else, he started to open up a little box on his little nightstand. It was like the ones that you got in the jewelry store, and immediately I knew what it was. I started to gasp, my body going crazy with excitement. I already knew what it was before he proffered it, and I got butterflies in my stomach just thinking about it.

"Wait. You don't mean me, do you?" I asked aloud. There was no way a guy like him could fall for me. Just no fucking way.

"Yes, you. I want you Farah, and I love you. I want to ask you to be my mate, and I also want to ask you to be something more than just a sexual partner to me. I want to ask you for your hand in marriage," he replied.

I didn't know what to say. I never thought this day would come. I honestly thought I was either going to die a lonely old widow or married to a man I fucking hated. I never thought I would get to feel that emotion called love, but here I was. I finally got to feel it, and I loved the way that it felt. It was magical, and I wanted it more and more with each passing second.

"How could I say no to you Tristan? You saved me, and you helped me realize that there is more to life," I replied.

That was an understatement, to say the least. Tristan showed me that I could be part of something more, and I would be able to really have a great life. I never thought that I could, but now that it's real I was more than happy to have it and accept it. And I know that I loved it as well. I loved this man, and I was not going to ever say no to something like this.

"So is that a yes?" he asked. He was dumbfounded by the sheer idea of it, and I know that things were going to be a whole lot better for us. This was the start of something new, and I meant that in the best way possible.

"Of course, I accept it, Tristan. I will marry you," I replied.

He smiled a giant grin that I had never seen on him before. It was the cutest goddamn thing ever, and it made my heart melt just by seeing it. He immediately grasped my hand and placed it on my ring finger, and I got a chance to check it out. It was simply perfect, and I loved how huge it was. The diamond was impressive, but the ring was something that was fit for a queen. I never thought that it was going to be something like this.

"Wow. This is amazing," I said.

"Well, I only wanted the best for you, babe," he said.

I immediately blushed at his words. Ever since we

started officially dating we actually were very fluffy and cute together. The rest of the pack thought that it was adorable, but sometimes I did feel a bit nervous about various things. Of course, those things were more sexual in nature, and I definitely didn't like doing anything of that sort in front of them.

"Aww," I replied.

However, our cute little fluffiness was immediately interrupted by a desire for each other. I felt so excited and happy that I was going to be his wife, and I could not control myself. I picked the winner, and he happily picked me.

He started to move himself closer to me until our lips were only inches apart. I liked feeling his breath on my lips, and I loved the way his beautiful eyes looked at me. His green eyes mesmerized me, and I already could feel my heart pounding and the lust present in my body. I could feel my panties getting wet just by looking at him, and the desire that I had for him was super strong and I could feel myself unable to control my desires for much longer.

"I want you," I said.

"I want you too," he replied.

We started to move our lips on top of each other, both of us engulfing each other in a passionate kiss. I loved feeling his lips against mine, and it was an amazing feeling. I loved the way we seemed to fit into each other's mouths perfectly, and as we continued to massage each other's tongues, I moaned in a wanton pleasure for him. I wanted to feel more, and already I could feel my body craving for him and wanting him even more.

He started to push me down, and I could immediately feel the skirt and shirt that I had started to discard. I started to pull off his own shirt and shorts and soon we were making out in his bed in our underwear. I smiled when we did this. I felt like a teenager again just making out with him. He made me feel young, and that was the best feeling ever and I loved it a whole lot.

He started to move his lips down my body, tracing them over to where my breasts were. He immediately pulled them out of my bra and started to swirl his tongue around the nipple, causing me to moan and arch my back in plea- sure. He smiled at me with a mischievous grin as he continued to do this, and already I could feel my breath hitching at the way this felt. This was the most amazing pleasure ever, and I couldn't imagine what to do next. I just wanted him, and I could tell from his hungry kisses and the way that he made me feel when he touched me that he wanted me as well.

He started to lightly move his finger against my other nipple, causing me to moan and arch my back in pleasure. He continued to do that, and already I could feel myself gasping for air at the sheer force of the pleasure bubbling up in my body. I wanted him so badly, and I know that he wanted me as well.

Of course, this time he wanted me to give him a little dosage of pleasure before we did anything else. I saw him start to undo his pants, but instead of putting it by my entrance, he placed it near my mouth. Soon his exposed cock appeared, and it was right by my lips.

I hadn't ever sucked his dick before, and I was a bit nervous about it. However, I decided to take it slow and take it all the way in. I started with the simple and innocent lick- ing, which made him Goran in pleasure as I did that. I then started to move my tongue against the bottom of the shaft, causing him to gasp in pleasure at the force of it. I smiled; I loved the way the man seemed to go crazy just by me lightly touching it. I went back up to the tip and started to lick the precum emitting out of it. Tristan moaned as I started to slowly move myself in there, taking it all in my mouth and reaching the back of my throat.

I started to gasp as I started to move myself up and down on him, the sound of my lips and the groans and moans the only sounds that were around. It was erotic, and I loved hearing it. However, I know that he was close already and I didn't want him to come just yet. I wanted to come with him.

I pulled myself off his cock and he looked at me with curiosity. I simply smiled and pointed to my pussy, which was already wet with pleasure.

"Let's come together," I said.

He smiled and moved himself down to where my pussy was, spreading my legs a little bit and causing me to shudder with the sudden air change. He then pushed himself into me, and soon he was moving in and out of me fast. I had never gone at this pace before, but immediately I started to moan in a wanton pleasure as he did this. It was so amazing, and the way he penetrated me was different from before. This time it was the best feeling ever, and I wanted him to continue. He thrust even harder and I could already I could feel my climax coming. After three more thrusts, I let out a loud moan as I let my pussy walls tighten against him. That was enough to send him over the edge as well, and soon I felt his cock twitch inside of my tight walls before he moaned, his cock emitting its own seed and filling up my pussy walls.

We were both spent at this point, and he pulled himself

out of me and moved next to me. He placed his hands around me and nuzzled my neck, causing me to giggle at the ticklish feeling. This was the best feeling ever, and I know that I chose the right man. I loved both of the alphas, but this was the one I wanted and cherished forever.

ABOUT THE AUTHOR

Candra Aubrey is an emerging erotica author of many erotica kinks and sub-genres. Be sure to check out other books and leave a review if this story got you hot!

Visit my blog at Candra Aubrey's Blog

Join my newsletter for the exclusive Candra Aubrey's Newsletter

Sign up for Free Stories from Xplicit Press Authors

Xplicit Press Author Updates

Like Xplicit Press on Facebook

Follow Xplicit Press on Twitter

Readers: I want to expand a few of the stories to see where the characters can be explored further. If there are any of the stories that you would like to read more about again, I'd love to hear from you!

Keep In Touch
Candra Aubrey
info@candraaubrey.com